NEW HORIZONS

A Tale of Big Hearts, Adversity and a Glimpse of Who We Really Are

By

Michael Mathers

MAPLE
PUBLISHERS

New Horizons: A Tale of Big Hearts, Adversity and a Glimpse of Who We Really Are

Author: Michael Mathers

First Published in 2024

ISBN 978-1-83538-421-3 (Paperback)
    978-1-83538-423-7 (Hardback)
    978-1-83538-422-0 (E-Book)

Cover Design and Book Layout by:
    White Magic Studios
    www.whitemagicstudios.co.uk

Published by:
    Maple Publishers
    Fairbourne Drive, Atterbury,
    Milton Keynes,
    MK10 9RG, UK
    www.maplepublishers.com

A CIP catalogue record for this title is available from the British Library.

PREFACE

I have 3 people to thank for getting this project off the ground.

First, my greatest friend John Hursey, who really started this project for me and has guided me and encouraged my efforts all the way.

Second, Lucy Ross, who, with her superb typing skills and patience over my complete lack of computer skills, has been so positive.

Third, Charles Flint, who has maintained an interest in my new writing efforts and always offered to help.

CONTENTS

Chapter One

The Journey

It had been pouring rain for days.

Two bedraggled hens crouched down on Andy's doorstep. They might have sheltered anywhere, but they knew that titbits were likely here because the regularity of Andy's daily return assured them of extra food.

Andy could not understand why two of his neighbour's hens wouldn't return to their home coop at night – especially with winter coming on.

One afternoon before Andy got home, the owner of the nearby farm came looking for her stray chickens as she had noticed the decreasing number of hens and eggs in the coop.

When she saw two of her hens sitting on the bothy bench, she shooed them in the farm's direction, but they disappeared behind the hedge until she moved away.

They seemed to prefer perching on Andy's bench by his front door, although it wasn't ideal. Life was getting tougher, but both hens had decided that returning to their home coop on the farm would not happen.

In due course, Andy gave them names: Cassie and Kate. He even had regular conversations with them. What he did not know was how much they appreciated his friendliness, or that they had regular conversations with one another once he had closed his front door at night.

However, one particular evening when Andy returned late from watching a football match, he saw the hens shivering with cold, their feathers fluffed up as they tried to keep warm. His heart went out to them.

"Come inside," he said. "It's only a small one-room bothy but there'll be space enough for all of us."

The hens could not believe the invitation at first – a warm safe haven overnight!

Nevertheless, they were sometimes scolded for jumping up on the bothy dining table for some extra food. Cassie, in particular, could be rather naughty!

"You've got a brass neck," Andy would say as he shooed them off the table.

Everything was going OK until Kate – the worrier of the two – noticed a visit by three men (in black suits and carrying briefcases) who appeared to be measuring distances around the farm, and around the bothy. Kate sensed that there was a change in the air and began to worry silently.

One evening, as Kate and Cassie were walking through the kitchen to their evening perch, they noticed a strange sight through the open bathroom door.

Perched on the edge of the bath was a duck.

"What on earth is that?" asked Cassie, slightly alarmed.

"And what's it doing on the edge of the bath? It could fall in," Kate added. They decided to keep their distance.

When Andy returned from work, he told the hens, "You have a new friend. He's called Jerome, and he'll be around for a while – mostly in the bathroom. He is recovering from his injuries.

"I was cycling home when I saw him on the grass verge by the roadside. He's obviously been attacked by a buzzard. Though his injuries are not life-threatening, he has lost a lot of blood. He enjoys the water in the bath, so be kind to him, Cassie and Kate. He's been through a lot."

As the days passed, Jerome began to feel better and decided to venture cautiously out of the bathroom ... and into the living room where he came face to face with the hens.

They all looked at each other in silence.

"What kind of hen are you?" asked Cassie.

"I'm not a hen at all. I'm a duck who likes water," Jerome replied.

"Well, we don't!" said Cassie firmly. "But I can't see that as a problem. Fancy teaming up with us?"

"If I could!" answered Jerome. (He'd been rather lonely in the bathroom).

"Of course you can," both hens replied in unison. "Come and share some of our evening food!"

Now that the ice of strangeness had been broken, Jerome was overjoyed to spend time with his new companions. Soon, they were all chatting away during the night while Andy was deeply asleep.

As you know, Kate was a worrier and got more concerned when Cassie asked questions about the future.

When she saw a strange cockerel, it was she who asked, "What are you doing perched on our bench?!"

The cockerel – who seemed a kind sort of soul – apologised and said, "My name is Tattie, and I'm just resting here before I move on to a better life. I hope I'm not intruding but you, too, need to ask questions about your future. I've heard that this farm will soon become a building site. What will there be to eat around here when houses are built? Especially with winter coming on. Nevertheless, can I stay with you a short while?"

The next time the postie brought letters, she brought news about the proposed new housing and asked Andy what he thought.

(The hens overheard the postie telling Andy that the farm, and therefore his little bothy, was destined to be pulled down to make way for a housing estate. Now they knew for sure that their future would be very different).

"I've been offered a flat in a block by my forestry employers, but I don't fancy living with lots of other people. After thirty years of being surrounded by wildlife – to say nothing of my lovely friends who visit, well ..." confessed Andy.

"Oh, come on!" laughed the postie. "You can't let a few birds rule your life!"

"I know what you're saying, but it all symbolises what I value about living here. Even so, if the building is to start soon, I have thought of applying for a warden's post on Stelling Isle on the west coast," said Andy, trying to sound calm.

"Well, you need to get a move on because I've heard the building is starting soon," the postie told him.

That evening, Andy talked aloud to himself as he tried to resolve the best thing for him to do. That was how all the birds knew for certain that their days of perching on the front bench were over.

The very next day, Andy searched for the advert about Stelling Isle before phoning for more information about the post.

"Yes," replied the administrator, "the post remains unfilled. And yes, you are well qualified for the role and have so much experience.

"How soon could you attend an interview? Next Monday? That would be fine."

A week later, when the postie delivered his letters, Andy told her the new address he was moving to in ten days. And yes, he did intend on taking his menagerie with him in his van.

"Time to get up hens, we've a long day ahead of us," said Andy softly. Cassie and Kate were still asleep, roosting on Andy's guitar amplifier. It would have to stay, the van was already full.

Everything was ready so they all jumped into the van, Andy driving and the hens – in a small wooden box lined with one of Andy's old jerseys – near the back doors. From there they could see the road ahead and Andy.

Leaving the bothy, they passed the bulldozers and other demolition equipment waiting for the van to leave. Time is money in their world and the bothy, in an hour, would be reduced to a dusty heap of rubble and removed from the site in huge skips.

Andy was glad to get away but tinged with sadness at leaving Jerome and the new cockerel behind. He had intended asking them to come with him, and yesterday, he searched around the bothy for them but to no avail. They had disappeared.

The large demolition engines roared into life as the van passed. Andy didn't look back. His new life with the hens on the Isle of Stelling had begun!

They were making good time; the hens were chattering away with one another. They also told Andy, who was fluent in hen language, about the new cockerel he had seen for a short while. According to Kate, his full name was King Tattius III, of noble Roman blood, who had met him in a large coop a few years ago.

He was a wise old bird and greatly loved by all the other hens. He asked only to be known as Tattie and it had been a joy having him as a leader. Again, a pang of regret pierced Andy. It was a mystery! He and Jerome had just disappeared!

Andy had been driving but a few hours when he sensed the happy chattering of Cassie and Kate changed to one of alarm.

"What on earth's the matter, hens?" said Andy without taking his eyes off the road.

"Andy! Andy!" blurted out the hens in a very agitated state. 'Your two jackets here in the back are moving on their own!"

"Don't be ridiculous," replied Andy. "How can two jackets move on their own?"

"But they are!!" said Cassie. "Look!"

Andy pulled into a layby and turned round to be met by his two jackets, one on either side of the hen box, visibly moving about!

Then, all of a sudden, two heads appeared from underneath the jackets. Jerome and Tattie!! They had hidden away, fearing they'd be left behind, not realising Andy had other plans for them.

Andy's cup of joy was overflowing. He realised now how much they all meant to him.

"Don't be silly!" said a small voice from beyond. "They're just birds."

Well, I don't care! replied a louder inner voice. *I love them all dearly. And you can just sod off!!*

They all had some food in the layby and then the journey resumed, all four chattering happily away. It felt so good to be back together again. But as they headed west, dark clouds were building up ahead.

Very shortly, the rain started, and as they got closer to the west, it got heavier and heavier. Soon, the narrow roads began to flood. The van wipers were going full tilt but could barely cope with the downpour. What happened next happened so quickly and unexpectedly that it seemed unreal and dreamlike to Andy.

The jarring thud as the front wheel hit a submerged pothole. The bang as the van's rear door flew open. The cries from the back as the hen box slipped out of the back of the van onto the flooded road, slid down the bank and floated away down the swollen stream that bordered the road.

He got out, just in time, to see two horrified hens looking out of the box as it caught the current and disappeared quickly, closely followed by a duck flapping its wings and paddling furiously to try and keep up and a large cockerel half flying, jumping and scrambling along an embankment, impossibly rough for any human to follow.

Andy just stood there in the rain, soaking wet, numb with shock. His last glimpse of the whole unbelievable episode was the look of terror and disbelief on Cassie and Kate's faces as they disappeared around a bend in the stream.

Andy knew that to follow in this rough west coast terrain was suicide. He didn't know how long he stood there in the rain, soaking wet. A blackness descended on him and enveloped his whole being, impenetrable, dense. His great friends were gone, just like that! True friends, loving friends! What a cruel twist of fate.

Somehow, Andy managed to get back into the van. It was all dense, opaque blackness. He just sat. Not thinking, numb to his soul. Then suddenly, unexpectedly, a tiny, brilliant speck of white light appeared from the depths of this darkness, piercing the blackness and getting stronger.

His inner vision saw it clearly. Then his head filled with white light just for a split second and two words. LOST and FOUND. What did it mean??

It didn't matter. He had a new job to go to. He put the van into gear and, with a heavy heart, set off again to Stelling Isle. His blackness started to lift as the heavy rain passed and the sun came out. Within one hour, he would be there.

"I can't hold it!" shouted Jerome as he desperately tried to hold onto the hen box and guide it out of the strong current into the shallows of what was not a fast-flowing river. He tried and tried again, but the grip of his beak was getting weaker as exhaustion set in. It was no use. His valiant rescue attempt seemed in vain. Cassie and Kate were rigid with fear and panic and couldn't move an inch in a box that was letting in water and quickly becoming waterlogged. It all seemed so hopeless!

Cassie and Kate could see Tattie farther downstream, perched precariously on a stone, waving his cockerel wings frantically as a thunderous roar began to develop and was getting louder.

As they passed him, out of reach, he shouted frantically at them, "Cassie! Kate! There's a large waterfall a short distance ahead! You've both got to fly to the bank. You've got to!"

"We can't fly!" they both shouted back in unison.

"You can fly, you're birds!" yelled Tattie.

"We don't know how to fly!" they both yelled back as they swiftly passed the rock.

"You must! You must!" shouted Tattie, but his words were lost in the roar of the approaching waterfall. All Tattie and Jerome could do now was to look on in horror as the box with Cassie and Kate arrived at the top of the waterfall, got caught on a large stone for a moment, and got swept over the edge. In total panic and without thinking, Cassie and Kate launched themselves in the air and FLEW!!! – or rather glided away down to the far bank.

"We can fly! We can fly!" they shouted triumphantly as the box disappeared down below and smashed into a thousand pieces as it hit the rocks.

And to think that a few seconds before, Cassie and Kate had been in it!

"Ouch!" said Kate as she landed roughly and hit the base of a tree. "Who put that there?" But she was okay, as was Cassie who landed with a bump close by. Jerome and Tattie arrived shortly, too. All four were back together in one piece although their feathers were rather wet.

They sat close together in silence, so happy to be alive with dear friends. Wise old Tattie had 'come up trumps again' with his 'Leap of Faith' encouragement for the hens. Everyone had given their all, and the nightmare was now over.

He decided to 'gather the troops' and plan a course of action. Jerome, Cassie and Kate were sitting, recovering from their ordeal.

"I suggest," he continued, "that we try to find Andy. Beaks up or down?"

All three beaks went up without hesitation.

"Right, that's settled. I've been thinking about this and I have a rough plan. Do we all want to find Andy?"

"Yes!" they all shouted in unison. "But we've no idea where he is," quacked Jerome.

"Well, we don't, but I picked up a few clues back at the bothy," Tattie began. "Firstly, I'm pretty sure we were going to the west coast to a place called Stelling Isle, whatever that is. I would hear him speak about it often."

"Yes, we heard him mention that place as well," they echoed.

"I really don't know what that is but I do know that it's on the coast somewhere and I also know that rivers go to the coast so I propose following this river as far as it goes. What say you all?"

They all agreed, without hesitation, to follow the river to its end and eat what they could on the way. There would be plenty of river plants for Jerome and worms and other beasties for the others.

They all set off with new hope. Sometimes, one bank was impossible to walk or they would just fly over to the other one. At night, for safety, they would roost in a tree. This was difficult for Jerome but the others would always help him up. So their unforeseen adventure continued! They knew that as the river got wider, the coast was getting closer and the mystery of Stelling Isle would hopefully be resolved.

The first day passed uneventfully. They would ask the occasional friendly bird if they had heard of Stelling Isle but always the same negative answer. One bird, a Great Spotted Woodpecker, seemed very friendly. He would drum on trees with this amazing beak and get food for them all.

"Do you not get a headache with all that pecking?" asked Tattie. Woody looked at Tattie with a puzzled expression.

"Of course not!" replied Woody. "I'm a Woodpecker!!" His beak could be a formidable weapon as well but he liked them all immensely. He had been a bit lonely but would never admit it. "Can I come with you all?" he finally asked.

"Of course you can," they all replied, and he became a firm friend.

Things can change quickly in life and thus it happened here.

Near the river they could see the edge of the wood and what looked like a cornfield. They decided to investigate. Tattie and the hens especially liked corn. They dropped their guard unconsciously – a fatal error!

All three were gorging on the lovely grain. No one was on guard. Woody and Jerome were at the river close by. They were being watched by unseen eyes. Mr Fox could see an easy meal before him. He was well hidden until he sprang into action!

In a flash, he had Kate in his mouth and was running off with her as she screamed her head off when Woody, who had heard the commotion, landed right on top of the fox's head, got his lethal beak into gear and battered Mr Fox's head.

"Ouch! I didn't expect this!" Mr Fox roared in pain as he dropped Kate. He beat a hasty retreat but not before turning round to Tattie with a vicious bite. He ran off. There would be other meals available that were not so temperamental!

Kate was more or less okay, but Tattie lay there gasping for breath, badly injured. He barely managed to sit himself up against a tree. They all did their best to make him comfortable but they knew the end was near.

Tattie saw his great friends through glazed eyes. All pain had gone now. Faintly, in the distance, he could see someone coming towards him. As she came closer, he recognised this beautiful, white speckled hen. It was his mother!

Everything was as clear as a bell. "Mother, how good it is to see you!" he cried, overcome with love.

"Yes, Tattie, it's been a while," she replied softly. "It's time," she said and she held his wing with hers and gently led him away. He glanced back, only for a second, to see an old cockerel lying motionless on a bed of moss surrounded by birds, friends, glowing with light.

The friends found a lovely, peaceful spot by the river to place Tattie's body. They stood in silence for a short while around it and then moved on.

The very next day the river began to taste different – salty – as they approached the coast. By the afternoon it had widened and merged with the ocean.

The birds arrived underneath a coastal bridge. Above was an X-road and some signs.

"Can anyone understand human-write?" asked Cassie. No one could. But when Kate mentioned Stelling Isle to Woody he recognised the word, being local. "Do any of these signs say Stelling Isle?" asked Cassie.

"I think possibly that's the one," replied Woody hesitantly, "but I'm not 100% sure."

"What do you, others, think?" asked Kate.

"I feel we should go for it," said Jerome and Cassie agreed. They all had a strange feeling that was the way to go and, after a few miles, arrived at a long concrete bridge. In fact, it was the causeway to Stelling Isle. Their inner guidance had been correct. Was wise old Tattie still about somehow?

Cassie and Kate decided to hide in some dense undergrowth next to the causeway while the good flyers, Jerome and Woody, could explore up ahead.

An hour passed. Nothing! Another hour passed. Nothing!

"Oh dear," murmured Kate. "What's happened to them?"

"There's no way of telling," replied Cassie, "but I feel it's okay."

Half an hour later Jerome and Woody arrived back.

"Great news hens! It is Stelling Isle and I think I recognised Andy's van outside a small croft cottage about one mile from the local shop. I don't think it's a very big island," he added.

The hens were ecstatic with the great news. "We may be together yet!" cried Cassie. What joy they all felt after their traumatic journey. The end was in sight!

"We're not there yet," piped up Woody, the newest member of the band. "We still have to be cautious; remember back there when we dropped our guard...?"

"Fair point," said Cassie.

"In the west here, there are plenty of large birds with fierce-looking beaks flying about ready and willing to make a meal of us," continued Woody. "So I suggest we lie up here, in this thick undergrowth, for the night and go for it tomorrow."

Everyone agreed.

Andy admitted to himself that, despite the kindness of Graham the shopkeeper and his new employers, he had lived 'under a cloud' this week, his first week on Stelling Isle. But he had finally come to terms with the loss of his great bird friends and moved on. Still, he would always have a special place for them in his heart.

Today he had a good day at work and was sitting on his veranda, not long back and enjoying a nice, strong coffee with honey and cream. He had all the 'bad habits' he chuckled inwardly.

The view was exceptional. The weather was set fair and he was enjoying a glorious view down the island glen and across to the shimmering peaks of the Inner Hebrides. Wow! They certainly didn't get any such views in the east!

What's that? Andy said to himself. *I must be imagining things.* About half a mile down the glen where the track appeared, he noticed some movement but he couldn't make out what it was. It was too far away.

Then, suddenly, a Great Spotted Woodpecker landed on his veranda and started tapping with its beak on one of his chairs. Then a large Mallard Duck quickly followed.

It couldn't be! "It can't be! Not Jerome surely?" Andy gasped.

"Hello Andy, we're back," quacked Jerome, as excited as Andy.

"Jerome," choked Andy. "I can't believe it!   Are the other .... ?"

"They're coming up the track," replied Jerome. "They'll be here in a minute."

Ah, thought Andy, *so that had been the movement down the track.*

Jerome jumped onto Andy's lap and Andy, now in seventh heaven, stroked his feathers tenderly, his eyes filling with tears. And finally Cassie and Kate appeared, saw Andy and ran the rest of the way in a sublime frenzy.

They jumped up onto his shoulder, feeling his warmth again and loving it. Andy was overcome with emotion; tears flowed freely, as Cassie and Kate told him the whole story of their river adventure, including Tattie's sad demise.

Andy 'came back to earth' then but, like the others, he felt Tattie's presence around them. His great friends were back. And they were all back together again.

What a joy!

YES! Truly LOST and FOUND!

Time eventually returned. Emotions levelled off to a warm, intimate glow and things settled down.

Woody was introduced and loved instantly, and everyone happily chatted away, recounting their adventures on the way. It would take all evening to fill in the details!

Andy said they could sleep anywhere in Ivy Cottage for one night only—on his bed if they wanted, but only for one night. It would all be sorted out in the morning. But the birds knew all about Andy's soft heart, and they also knew that his rules could be broken very easily.

Later in the evening, everyone drifted off to sleep in a misty haze of happiness. It was great to be back together. It had been a long while!

Chapter Two

Stelling Isle, Sticky Toffee Pudding and Schuberts Impromptu

Stelling Isle wasn't a large island, being only six square miles and loosely oval in shape. Like several west-coast islands, it generally sloped down from west to east and the Atlantic Ocean had carved many precipitous gullies and inlets over the millennia, mostly in its western edge.

The sheltered eastern edge, where the recent causeway had been built, held Stelling Village which, at one time was supplied from the mainland by a small but very hardy little ro-ro ferry. It always ran across the short stretch of water between Stelling Isle and the mainland, except in periods of very bad weather. Now it sat, sad and neglected, on the beach next to Stelling Harbour.

The village residents these days were a mixture of the old native crofters, inshore fishermen and new residents from the south, but everyone got on well together.

Dotted around the rest of the island were a few crofts whose main income was from sheep farming. Sheep roamed everywhere and it wouldn't be the first time Andy had risen early only to find lambs tucking into his delicious plants and privet hedging while others would lie at his door and on his veranda, not looking very phased by his half-hearted attempt to shoo them off! They seemed to sense his deep love of all God's creatures and acted accordingly!

The local shop's new owner was a lovely man called Graham. He'd only shortly arrived: a senior gentleman from the south who had kindly donated, free of charge, a week's supply of food when Andy had arrived. He had a seriously wicked dry sense of humour which Andy found hilarious, and he took a dram! Quite a character! As was his dog Florence, a show cocker spaniel who held herself with a regal gait but was so friendly to all.

All the birds – Cassie, Kate, Jerome and Woody – had settled in well after their river adventures. Andy rebuilt the hen house round the back which had originally been a shed in days gone by but, more often than not, they slept with Andy in the cottage not heeding his weak, unconvincing protestations!

They all missed Tattie but his presence could still be felt during any quiet period. What a bird!

The newest member of the happy band, Woody, could on occasion be rather naughty. An example of this was when he got his beak stuck in one of Andy's home-made sticky toffee puddings despite being warned not to go near it! What a commotion! Andy heard the panicky wing beats and muted bird shrieks coming from the kitchen and went through immediately.

"Woody! I warned you against sticking your beak into that sticky toffee pudding, didn't I?"

Woody was speechless. Well, in fact, he couldn't speak with his beak firmly wedged into a piece of toffee at the back of the pudding. If a Great Spotted Woodpecker could blush, Woody would've gone bright red, but he only spoke after Andy had carefully extracted his beak from the pudding.

"I'm so sorry," said Woody. "I know I said I wouldn't but it was too tempting and I can resist anything but temptation!"

"Well, you've only got yourself to blame," answered Andy trying to sound stern and failing miserably. "You are a Great Spotted Woodpecker, are you not Woody? And your beak is designed for drilling and pecking into timber to get food. It is definitely <u>not</u>, I repeat <u>not</u>, designed for eating home-made sticky toffee pudding. Agreed?" Andy was now having great difficulty in stifling an attack of loud belly laughter!

"Yes Andy, I'm sorry. I completely agree. I don't know what came over me. Please don't send me away, I couldn't bear it," said Woody, getting upset.

"I would never do that Woody, you can be sure of that," replied Andy. "I love you dearly as do all the other birds. We will always be together and that will always include you! We just have to accept our weaknesses and move on. What you resist persists, Woody! Always remember that. Now, are you okay?"

"Yes Andy," replied the crest-fallen bird.

"Good, good! Now, where are the others?"

"Outside," said Woody.

"So why not go outside and join them while there's still light?"

"Great idea!" said Woody and hopped outside in a much better state of mind.

Later in the week, the birds became more adventurous and explored farther and farther away from Andy's croft. Woody knew of the 'hooky beak' danger and emphasised that fact to the others.

"It's safe enough around these parts, but we have to be careful. Remember Mr Fox!"

How could they forget?

Jerome loved all the water about and, although he was a fresh-water duck, was starting to get used to the salt water as well. Cassie and Kate were also enjoying their newly discovered ability to fly short distances. They would launch themselves off a rock outcrop at the back of Ivy Cottage and glide, sometimes for half a mile, until landing on some soft sphagnum moss.

They both loved that feeling of being completely free in the air and were also getting better and better at it. *Why hadn't we tried this years ago?* they wondered. Thankfully, they had forgotten the purgatory of the battery-hen life they had survived when young.

One day after work, Andy realised that he needed some provisions. He knew that time was getting on as he glanced at his watch. The shop would've just closed but Graham had always said that, unofficially, he would stay open well into most evenings if anyone was desperate.

Andy decided to go down in his van as the light faded. As he arrived, he thought he could faintly hear some piano music and it seemed to be coming from the back of the shop. He stopped in his tracks and listened again. He thought he recognised it. It sounded classical like a Schuberts Impromptu, a piece he had heard before and loved.

"Yep, that's it," he said softly to himself. And it was being played beautifully. As he went to the door a bell sounded, the music stopped, and Graham appeared at the counter.

"Hello Andy, what can I do you for this evening?" he asked with his familiar gusto.

"Do you play the piano?" asked Andy.

Graham looked a bit embarrassed. "A bit," he replied. "I used to be pretty good years ago but that was then," he added, blushing slightly.

"A bit?!" replied Andy aghast. "I recognised that piece of music you were playing just now. It's a Schuberts Impromptu. I used to play it all the time on my record player and you were playing it amazingly well. I have a good musical ear, you know, so don't deny it!"

"Thanks Andy, much appreciated. Anyway, can I help you with any provisions?" He had quickly changed the subject. Andy picked up the signal and said no more.

With his needs supplied, Andy decided that such talent shouldn't go unnoticed and made a mental note to follow it up sometime in the future.

Chapter Three
Florence & Jimmy

Sometimes Florence, Graham's 'royal' Cocker Spaniel, would come up the road after she had made sure things were okay with Graham at the shop. She would mix with her friends at Ivy Cottage for a short while and just enjoy their lovely company.

They could see she was royalty and enjoyed kidding her about it!

"I'm surprised you mix with us mere commoners, Florence! We must thank you for your 'Royal Presence'! What an honour it is for us!!"

"Yes, well," Florence would reply. "One has to mix with one's subjects at times. It is rather demeaning for me, personally, but one has to make allowances for those of 'common descent', doesn't one?!"

Nobody, royalty or otherwise, could then prevent the air being filled with a cacophony of deafening animal and bird laughter which echoed down the glen. They all loved Florence, and she loved them.

A fortnight later, after her morning duties at the shop had been completed, she was up again enjoying the company at Ivy Cottage when suddenly two sheep ran straight past her in a panic, rushed through the gate and into the back garden. Florence was chatting to Woody at the time and they both saw a dog fast approaching. She stood firmly at the gate blocking any further entry. The dog 'jammed on the anchors'!

"Get out of my way spaniel, I'm going in!" shouted the evil-looking mongrel, teeth bared and ready to bite.

"Hold on, Sir!" replied Florence. "What is your business here?"

"No business but my business, you, stupid dog. Now, I'll say this for the last time – get out of my way! I'm going to enjoy biting and worrying those sheep, so shift or I'll bite you!"

Florence never flinched. "Dear, dear! There is no need for this, young man." She glanced at Woody perched on the wooden gate. He looked menacing for the first time, calmly sharpening his beak on the gate post. His silent message was obvious – *You Dare!*

"My dear dog, I abhor violence of any sort," said Florence. "It is the way of the Ignorant. There are many other paths one can take. You look to me like a very handsome dog so let's talk before anyone gets hurt."

"No, I'm a mongrel! Everyone says I'm ugly and a monster and they don't like me. So now I know I'm a monster and do things that monsters do like biting humans and sheep and plenty more!"

"My dear, dear dog. You are <u>not</u> a monster and never were a monster. The monster in you was created by other people telling you constantly that you were a monster. So eventually you believed it and became one. I am Royalty, so take this as fact! You are not and never were a monster. You are a very handsome dog, believe me, I wouldn't lie about it! Please tell me your name, Sir, I would love to know. Maybe we could even become friends and, oh! By the way, you've got a lovely set of front teeth as well."

Jimmy, for that was his name, just stood, dumbfounded and silent for once in his life. He'd never been spoken to like that before and yet it all rang true! All he'd heard throughout his life was Monster! Monster! Monster! Monster! Maybe it wasn't true at all!

He just sat on his haunches in a trance, all menace gone. Florence came up and gave him a paw which he graciously and gently licked, then he turned slowly and walked back down the hill.

"Jimmy!" He turned around. "Please come and visit us again. We'd love to see you," barked Florence and Jimmy's cup overflowed with love and acceptance, the only true healers.

He was a different dog now!

Chapter Four

Who Are You?

Now it was high summer on Stelling Isle and all life was taking advantage of the long warm summer nights and the mild summer breezes.

Cassie and Kate were laying almost one or two eggs each day. Woody was making frequent visits to the mainland to enjoy days of pecking on rotten trees with the reward of delicious bugs and beasties. Trees were rare on Stelling Isle. He always returned promptly in the evening before it got dark so no one worried!

Only Jerome was acting strangely. "Where have you been today, Jerome?" Andy would ask but Jerome was not forthcoming, keeping things 'close to his breast'.

He always replied with a, "Nowhere special. Just up at the cliffs, looking about."

Andy was puzzled. This went on for a few more days before Andy decided to get to the bottom of it.

"Jerome!" he said. "Tell me what's going on. We're great friends, aren't we?"

"Of course we are!" quacked Jerome sincerely. "Okay, I'll tell you. Could you come with me, sometime soon, to the western cliffs of the island? There's a cove I have to take you to."

"What? Why Jerome? Why? Who says!?"

"I'm not sure, I don't know why," answered Jerome. "All I know is that I have to ask you to come, that's all! I don't know any more," he whined, getting slightly upset.

Andy knew that Jerome was a very sensitive bird and could be easily upset so he lowered his voice and softened his tone as much as possible.

"We've been through a lot, you and I, Jerome, haven't we? Remember that roadside grass verge and buzzard? That's where we first met, wasn't it?" said Andy.

"Oh yes, how could I forget? I thought I was a goner!" reflected Jerome.

"But you weren't, were you? And we've been together ever since. Look at you, Jerome, you're the most handsome Mallard Duck I've ever seen. That's honest! I would never part with you," said Andy softly. "So tell me what this is all about."

"Thanks Andy," said Jerome, now completely relaxed.

"Well, I've been speaking to someone up at the western cliffs who I somehow seem to vaguely recognise. He can speak Duck and he says he knows you. He would like to speak to you and he told me where to go, but Andy!" Jerome hesitated, lost for words. "He's both there and he's not there! That's it! I can't explain it anymore, I just don't understand."

Andy could see Jerome was getting upset again. He himself didn't understand it either, but he calmed everything down a second time. "Of course I'll go with you, Jerome," and he meant it. He trusted Jerome implicitly, and they decided to go that weekend if the weather was fair.

The weekend duly arrived and, although Saturday was dull and misty, Sunday dawned bright and sunny. Andy was making breakfast with a view to sitting out in the early morning sun while Cassie, Kate, Jerome and Woody were chatting away on the veranda. He smiled inwardly when he overheard Jerome proudly boasting to Woody that he, Jerome, was a water bird and could happily float and paddle on water and even, briefly, swim below it if he so desired!

"Bet you can't do that Woody, eh?" he boasted, proudly puffing out his breast feathers.

"Hmm! That's true Jerome, I certainly can't do that," replied Woody with a twinkle in his eye, "but I could peck a hole right through you with my beak, Jerome, in about thirty seconds! Bet you couldn't do that?!"

"Ah, touché!" cried Jerome, "I am humbled!" and they both laughed heartily and continued eating their breakfast. They were great friends.

Andy decided to go to Jerome's cove after breakfast. It was all a bit of a mystery but he liked mysteries so now was the time.

"Can I come as well, Andy?" asked Woody. "I won't get in the way."

"Of course, you can," replied Andy. "I don't actually know why we're going but I feel I have to for some reason."

Woody was slightly puzzled but trusted Andy's intuition implicitly. "Can I perch on your shoulder when we go, Andy? I'd love that!" continued Woody.

"Yes, of course, Woody. You know you don't have to ask," came the soft reply. Andy had absolutely no favourites but Woody, who could be rather naughty sometimes, was a great character.

After breakfast they set off. Cassie and Kate decided to stay behind. They were both laying, on average, two eggs a day now and in between times they continued to practise their flying and gliding skills. Their hen coop – clean, bright and very pleasant to roost (when they weren't lying on Andy's bed!) was such a joy. Gone were the dark, satanic days of their previous smelly, dirty and damp existence. How they had survived those days (many hadn't) God only knows!

The wild mountain thyme and the fresh sea breezes mingled together to give a rich, intoxicating aroma as the three friends made their way to the island's west side. The view out across the Minch to all the islands beyond lifted the heart, and the sparkle of the sun dancing on the white-tops reminded Andy that the Garden of Eden was not an other-worldly place but right here, right now!

"There is no way I can climb down these cliffs, Jerome," remarked Andy when they finally arrived on the scene. "It would be suicidal to even try. I'm not and never will be a keen rock climber. If I can't walk down hills without ropes then it's a 'no go' for me! Sorry Jerome."

What he saw, down below, was a small pebble and rock cove with a small sandy beach at the far end. Very beautiful, but Andy couldn't see a way down. It was all sheer cliffs. "I'm not a bird, Jerome! I can't fly down," he said, disappointed.

"You don't have to fly down," said Jerome. "Follow me!" and they continued along the cliff-top towards a rough, rocky outcrop above the beach-end of the cove.

"What's the point in going any farther, Jerome?" asked Andy. "I'll have to climb over this outcrop and that won't be easy, never mind climbing down the cliff-face. It's impossible!!"

"It's okay, Andy, I know a way down for you," said Jerome surprisingly. "See that split in the rocks up ahead? Well, there's a sort of tunnel there, rough, but passable at low tide. It takes you all the way down to the bottom. I've done it but, remember, it's only possible at low tide, which is due shortly."

"Okay, Jerome, let's have a look," replied Andy with a feeling of misgiving. He was way out of his 'comfort zone' now but he tended not to be a quitter so he clambered up to the split in the rocks up ahead to get a closer look at what was there.

He found, to his surprise, that it was much more than a split in the rocks but rather a very rough tunnel which disappeared downhill at an angle not too acute for walking.

"Are you sure about this Jerome?" Doubt was setting in. "Woody, you can bail out if you want, I'm not sure about this," admitted Andy.

"If you're going, I'm going!" replied Woody and dug his claws deeper into Andy's jacket for extra support.

So they all climbed down slowly and carefully. At times, it was very narrow and at other times, very low, but eventually it opened up into a large cavern. As they entered it, Andy could see light at the other end. *Wow! It must be a cave!* Andy thought. They must've clambered down some sort of 'blowhole' at the back of the cave. He had heard of them; where the ocean creates an escape for its waves as it pounds the coast over eons of time, finding weaknesses in the rocks. The incessant pounding creates a channel venting at the top of a cliff, highly pressurised and quite spectacular. Almost like a whale venting through its 'Blow hole'!

Andy walked out of the cave with his birds and round to a lovely sandy beach beyond. "What a beautiful, peaceful place," he remarked. "Quite stunning!" And Woody and Jerome had to agree. They had trusted Andy implicitly and were reaping the rewards.

All three just stood silently, drinking it all in, enchanted!

Jerome was the first to speak. "We can easily fly back up to the top," he said. "We'll wait for you up there. You've got an appointment to keep in the cave, Andy."

"But how? Why?" Andy hesitated, but they were both gone. There was no answer!

He sat for a while, drinking in the eternal beauty of this natural land and seascape. It enveloped him in a softness that defied logic and extended way past thought. Something seemed to be opening up inside him. What was it? He had no idea.

He returned to the cave entrance and went in. It was much cooler there, and there he waited. For what? Again, he had no idea.

"Hello Andrew, how are you?"

Andy whirled around, caught unawares. There in front of him was a figure of a man. In the gloom he couldn't make out much detail but, impossibly, he felt that somehow he knew this person.

"Who are you? How did you get here?" he asked.

But the figure didn't seem to hear him.

"It's good to see you, Andrew, it's been a while." Andy somehow recognised the voice but couldn't just place it. "I know all about you, Andrew," said the figure in a calm, relaxing voice. "Remember your first scout camp at Glen Prosen in '66 when you climbed that big birch tree?"

"Yes, yes, how could I forget?" replied Andy. "Well, I suppose you know that I climbed to the top, stood on a rotten branch which broke and in an instant I fell."

"Yes, and what happened after that?" asked the figure softly.

"Well, to be truthful, I don't really know," replied Andy. "All I know is that I ended up standing on a lower branch way down near the bottom of the tree and I've no idea how I got there! Anytime I mention it to anyone, they don't understand and look at me as if I'm bonkers so I've stopped mentioning it to anyone because they don't believe me and maybe rightly. It does seem impossible, doesn't it?"

"That's true," said the figure. "But I believe you, Andrew, because I was there!"

"You were?" stammered Andy. Tears were welling up in his eyes. It had been many years ago. He had been only thirteen years old.

"We parted company then," continued the figure, "but we will always meet again because we are all much, much bigger than we think we are."

"Yes, we are One, my dearest friend."

Andy's head was bowed. Tears flowed freely and when he finally looked up the figure was gone. He looked around but to no avail. He had wanted, so much, to ask a million questions.

Had he imagined it all? He knew, deep down, he hadn't but no one would believe him anyway.

Some sea spray touched his forehead, gently reminding him that it was time to go. He looked out at the cave entrance. The ocean was much closer now. Definitely time to go! So he retraced his steps slowly but surely up the tunnel. A small, glowing ball of light led the way and at the entrance, merged with the All and disappeared.

"Thank you," said Andy silently.

Jerome and Woody were there to greet him as he emerged. "How did you get on? Did you see anyone? Come on Andy, tell us!" they cried in unison, keen to know what happened. But Andy just smiled a secret smile and tactfully changed the subject.

"You both look quite tired. Was it a difficult climb back up the cliffs?" asked Andy, so they chatted away about all the ledges they had to rest on and the other birds they met on the way up. Jerome looked particularly exhausted and asked to sit on Andy's other shoulder opposite to Woody.

"Of course you can, Jerome," agreed Andy, so they set off for home, Andy with a Mallard Duck on one shoulder and a Great Spotted Woodpecker on the other.

With Jerome having webbed feet, he often lost his balance as Andy carefully negotiated the rough terrain, thus Andy would get a periodic slap in the face by one of Jerome's wings as he tried to regain it.

"Jerome, I've got a better idea than my shoulder," quipped Andy with a wry smile. "Why don't I tighten the bottom cord of my jacket and open the zip half-way so you can then comfortably sit inside it with your head looking out. It would save me from getting slapped in the face every minute! What say you, Jerome?"

Jerome was all for it so the contented but weary trio wound their way back to Ivy Cottage in the early evening light. It had been some day!

Cassie and Kate were waiting to greet them, eager to hear the details of their clifftop adventure. But after a quick meal, Andy's eyes began to close as the weariness of the day made its mark, but not before it came to him, the answer to who the figure was in the cave; the answer he had been silently asking for all the way back.

Ah yes, he now knew!

In the early morning hours, as the sun's golden rays slanted across his room, Andy lay awake watching them move serenely across his bed. The silence of the new day was deafening. Peace lay with him as an understanding of yesterday deepened in his heart.

He remembered a school quote from Shakespeare:

There are more things in heaven and earth, Horatio,

than were ever dreamt of in your philosophy.

He hadn't understood it then but now it meant something. Yes, he understood a bit more!

Chapter Five

Dougal & Deism

L ife settled down into a happy routine for Andy and his birds. Routines help you along your chosen path, but if it develops into a rut then best to get out of it as soon as possible as there is only one way you are going and that is down!

Andy knew that from bitter experience at the bothy years ago. *No chance of that happening now*, he thought during an occasional pensive mood. He loved his birds too much and the locals on Stelling Isle were very friendly and helpful, yet he would never forget his strange, almost mystical cove experience.

Now, looking back, was it a dream? Was it real? It was real to him and that was the most important thing.

A new day arrived and he had work to do. The least enjoyable part was the paperwork. He loathed it but it had to be done! To Andy, it was a necessary evil, so he spent most of the morning in his tiny little office at the back of the cottage sorting everything out. It was really part of the old cowshed converted, and here he focused on the job at hand.

He was almost finished when he heard a knock on the door. It was never locked except in bad weather and he didn't get many visitors so he was a little surprised. He put his pen down and went to the door.

"Hello Reverend, what a surprise! Come in. The door's never locked," he added with a welcoming smile. "What brings you to these parts?"

There was no church in Stelling, but a mile over the causeway was the village of St Minnis which had a rather attractive little church set back from the village. It was protected from the worst of any bad weather by several rocky outcrops and the manse was close by.

"Hello, I'm Dougal Mackay the local minister. I suppose my 'dog collar' gives me away!" he said jokingly. "Stelling Isle is part of my remit so I thought I'd make a social call on you just to say hello and to invite you to a recital and social evening at St Minnis church hall in the autumn. Your neighbour, Graham Chertsey, has offered to play some piano and there'll be plenty to eat and drink afterwards. No one has really heard him yet, but he says that he used to play classical piano down south, so we asked him if he'd play. Everyone says he's a lovely man, very obliging."

"Sounds good," replied Andy. His thoughts returned to his first day on the island when all had gone wrong on the journey there. He wouldn't forget the week's groceries and the small card that greeted him as he opened the door for the first time. What a joy that had been and how it had helped to soothe his troubled heart after his traumatic journey from the east. He never looked back after that. The memory of this kindness never left him. He would always remember!

"Would you like a cup of tea, Reverend?" asked Andy.

"Oh, that would be lovely thanks, but just call me Dougal if you'd like. 'Reverend' sounds so formal doesn't it? And this is a social call!"

"That's fine by me, Dougal," Andy said and they shook hands. "I never heard your car arrive," added Andy. "You didn't walk, did you?"

"Och, no!" replied Dougal. "I thought I'd get some exercise and took the bike."

"Ah yes, good thinking, Dougal," said Andy. "And it's mostly downhill all the way back! Oh, I almost forgot. Would you like a wee dram to go with your tea, Dougal?"

"That would be lovely," said Dougal, his eyes lit up!

Andy knew a bit about the relationship between islanders and whisky. What others thought was a generous glassful of whisky was, to west coasters, just a damp glass! So Andy made sure he filled the glass almost to the brim. Dougal's eyes shone when he saw it but glazed over in increments as the glass slowly emptied.

"Are you sure you'll be alright on your bike, Dougal?" asked Andy when it was Dougal's time to leave.

"No problem, Andy!" replied an ever-so-slightly well-oiled Dougal. "I'll just point my bike downhill and switch to automatic. It'll go home itself!" he laughed.

Andy did a quick visual inspection of Dougal's pushbike. It had obviously seen 'better days' and Andy couldn't see any brakes at all!

"Thank you so much for the cup of tea and dram, Andy," said Dougal sincerely. "Maybe we'll see you at St Minnis some Sunday. If not, there's Graham's recital coming up. All the best!" and with a cheery wave, he set off down the hill. The bike wobbled alarmingly and before he was out of sight Andy saw the bike disappear into a roadside ditch, Minister and all!

Dougal looked over seventy and to be ruthlessly honest, had obviously eaten 'too many pies' over the years! So when Andy saw the bike disappear into the ditch it looked bad. He rushed out to his van, very concerned.

He should have worried! He found Dougal lying in the heather none the worse for his fall, humming an old Gaelic aire. Andy helped him up, saw he was okay and 'wedged' him into the van passenger seat. Not an easy job!

He examined Dougal's bike. It was surely a goner! Both wheels were so buckled they almost looked square and the frame was as bent as a banana! No way back for this bike, I'm afraid. It looked ancient so it had had a good life. Its remains went in the back of the van.

They drove off to the manse at St Minnis with Dougal now in full voice, singing in Gaelic without a care in the world. It was purgatory to Andy! It all sounded so very out of tune.

Thankfully the journey was short, the musical accompaniment ended and they arrived at the manse where a rather grim-faced housekeeper was there to greet them.

"You've been at the 'demon drink' again have you, Dougal?" she said sternly as they both helped him upstairs to his bed. It was only just past midday! Andy could now see he had a problem and made a mental note to call and see how he was doing in the not-too-distant future. Dougal's heart was in the right place, he could see that.

That afternoon, with the drudgery of the month's paperwork completed, Andy sat on the veranda with his dear bird friends and slipped into a pensive mood, something he rarely did these days.

Could he possibly go back and attend church services again as he had once done years ago?

Then, he had been a regular churchgoer and became an avid reader of anything religious or spiritual. He loved, on occasion, just sitting in a church in silence when no one else was around. He always felt something indefinable present. Something totally accepting, totally loving, much, much bigger than himself.

Much of what he felt seemed in conflict with orthodoxy. Surely, to Andy, conditional love was not love at all but a counterfeit version, a kind of oxymoron. *I'll love you if ... !?* it didn't make sense. He didn't feel he was on permanent probation either. In the end, he formed a view of a God who was wholly part of ... and not wholly separate from ... his creations and thus slowly and gradually slipped away from church attendance despite meeting some lovely people and hearing some amazing sermons that touched his heart.

But why not go again and listen? There was no harm in that. That was then, this is now!

So Andy decided to maybe give it a go again. Yes, why not? He loved churches, he loved sermons and he loved many churchgoers. He made another mental note.

❖

Chapter Six

Cassies CowDonkeys

The peace of Andy's afternoon reverie was shattered when Cassie and Kate barged onto the veranda in a fluttering state of panic.

"Andy! Andy! Two strange cows are causing chaos in the back garden, eating our grass and some of our flowers. Woody gave them a sharp peck in the behind and told them to get lost! But they're still here. They say they've got nowhere to go!"

"Okay, okay! Come on hens, calm down. I'm sure it's not that bad," replied Andy. "Let's have a look at them."

He walked around the back and was greeted by a very unusual situation. Woody, Cassie, Kate and Jerome were up in arms! Woody was threatening to peck them to bits. Jerome was quacking loudly and flapping his wings, trying to look threatening and really not succeeding, while the hens were clucking away at full volume. The strange cows weren't cows at all. They were two rather emaciated-looking donkeys who were clearly starving.

They were tucking in hungrily to the new grass. Some flowers were getting the chomp as well.

Andy approached slowly and cautiously, making no sudden movements. Several years ago he used to volunteer at a small local animal sanctuary and had gained quite a lot of experience with donkeys. They were not always the 'sweetie pies' one imagines them to be. Occasionally, they could be bad-tempered for some reason and then dangerous. Their bites were notoriously painful, but if you spent time with them and got through their hard outer shell, they were the most beautiful, loving, gentle animals in the kingdom. They were also very intelligent.

"Hello donkeys, how are you?" Andy enquired gently. No reply. He could speak a bit of Donkey but sometimes it was difficult getting through.

"That's tasty grass, I'll bet, isn't it?" continued Andy.

One donkey looked up. *A human was actually speaking to them in their own language!* she thought, *and so gently as well!* She'd never experienced that before. It was usually threatening shouts and warnings they received. "Look, we're sorry for intruding, but we're starving and this is such good grass."

"Where are you from?" enquired Andy but was interrupted by the squeal of brakes as an old Land Rover ground to a halt round the front and out jumped a middle-aged crofter with hard, non-compromising eyes which were aflame with anger.

"There you are!" he shouted angrily, "I've been after you two all day! When we get back, you'll both pay for this! It'll be the last time you escape!" He grabbed some rope out of his trailer with a view to capture and just strutted arrogantly into Andy's back garden without permission.

Cassie, Kate, Jerome and Woody flew at him. They disliked him intensely from the first moment he arrived. Woody went straight for his knees and after a few hard pecks, he went down 'like a sack of tatties'.

Jerome immediately jumped on his head and gave him a few good wallops with his strong wings, while Cassie and Kate finished the job with some hard pecks to his ears.

Bullies are always cowards deep down and this bully was no different! He yelped and squealed, jumped up and beat a hasty retreat to the safety of his Land Rover with the birds in hot pursuit.

Andy, a witness to all this, thought he'd better try and calm down the 'troubled waters'. During the commotion, he had decided what he was going to do.

"Hello," he said placidly, trying to defuse the situation as much as possible. "Sorry about the birds but they're not keen on sudden invasions of their own private space. Can I get you a glass of water or some plasters? You seem to have cut yourself in a few places when you tripped. The garden path can be treacherous if one is not careful – many apologies!" He looked the man straight in the eye.

"I didn't cut myself, you idiot, it was those birds that attacked me! You should have them done away with!" he snarled. "Anyway, I want my donkeys back. They can make money for me. Get them!"

"I don't think they want to go with you, I'm afraid. Isn't it obvious? Look! They're cowering in the far corner of the garden, aren't they?" replied Andy sharply. The bad-tempered crofter had to agree with that, but grudgingly so. "Look, I'll give you a fair price for them. They obviously don't like you and won't perform for you. I know donkeys! I'll give you two hundred quid for them both. I'd say that's more than a fair price, considering their condition. Is it a deal?"

"I suppose so. I don't like them anyway."

And they obviously don't like you, thought Andy. He was having a problem remaining courteous, so he went inside Ivy Cottage to his old bureau and got the cash, handed it over and watched the beat-up old Land Rover retreat down the hill and away.

Peace was restored and the two new additions to the family, seeing their previous owner leave, relaxed and settled down to eat some more delicious green grass.

You know, donkeys are a breed apart and very special. Over the centuries they've been known as 'beasts of burden' and have been used and abused by humans for so long. As a result, they've had to 'dig in' and 'soldier on' in their misery with almost super-human toughness, never flinching until the inevitable, cruel end.

Jesus rode into Jerusalem to his death, not on a shining white stallion but on a lowly donkey. Exalting them to the highest level.

That's why all true donkeys have 'The Cross of Christ' on their backs. Look closely and you'll see it! To get on well with donkeys is simple! Just apply a good dose of TLC and observe the results. Happy donkeys are a joy to see!

Andy named the donkeys Dave and Morag and they quickly settled into their new home. The birds loved them and got a great thrill when Dave and Morag would allow them onto their backs and give them a short ride around Ivy Cottage. The donkeys were so kind and gentle. Their previous horrible existence slipped rapidly into the past. Cassie especially loved them but got slightly confused one day when speaking to Andy.

"They really are lovely cows, Andy," said Cassie. Andy had been making supper and looked up, puzzled.

"No, Cassie! They're not cows; they're a type of horse!" he replied, trying not to laugh.

"We've never seen horses, but we've seen cows at the bothy in the field opposite," said Cassie, slightly confused. "They must be cows! They've got a tail and four legs like a cow and they eat grass like a cow, so they must be cows, Andy!"

Oh dear, how can I explain? Andy wondered. "Look, Cassie, you can call them cows if you want, but I'll try to get a picture of a cow and a horse, and then you can decide yourself which one they look like most. Is that not fair?"

"Oh, would you please Andy? But until then is it okay to call them cow-donkeys?"

"Of course you can, Cassie! Whatever you call them, they've definitely taken a shine to you, that's for sure," smiled back Andy, and Cassie went off, happy in the knowledge that Dave and Morag, 'the cow-donkeys' liked her very much!

The donkeys' emaciated bodies soon filled out as a result of being well-fed and well-liked. They were very happy now.

Chapter Seven

Wellbeing

It had been a long, hard winter on Stelling Isle. The unrelenting wind and rain seemed to go on forever, making everything and everyone continually wet. What a joy was Andy's peat fire! The smell of burning peat intoxicated the nostrils of man, beast and bird with its lovely rich aroma whilst its heat was a godsend for drying out wet clothes, feathers and hides.

The donkeys, Morag and Dave, lived in the hen coop with Cassie and Kate (and I know what you readers are thinking: donkeys can't fit into hen coops! It just isn't going to work, and you'd be right – they are far, far too small).

But, in fact, this coop was originally a shed when Ivy Cottage was a working croft. It was originally Ivy Croft Cottage that any mail was sent to. Gradually, over the years, the 'Croft' part was dropped after it ceased being a working croft and reverted to being a rented cottage.

So the 'coop' was quite spacious and, indeed, could comfortably hold Dave, Morag, Cassie and Kate, who just loved them being about overnight with them in the coop.

Yes, the donkeys did take up a lot of room, but Andy didn't mind that and neither did Cassie and Kate.

It was great to see them no matter what: Cottage or Coop!

Sometimes they just enjoyed lying, in peace, in the coop next to the hens and not one egg was ever pinched or broken.

Thankfully for all, the weather seemed to be easing, as confirmed by the forecast. Spring was upon them with her magical ways and the days were getting longer. Everyone could feel the earth coming alive again. She'd been asleep for what had seemed like an eternity.

Being spring, it was time for Andy to go around and inspect all the fences that were his responsibility and repair any the winter had played havoc with. Also, bird counts were required and a multitude of other jobs besides. So he was very busy! The birds and animals could sense this and were on their very best behaviour in order to reduce any stress to a minimum. They really loved him, and this was a practical and everyday way of demonstrating it.

They were also becoming more aware of the island's dangers when out and about. Nobody wanted any cliff-top accidents, did they?

One late morning, they were all in the back garden together, Andy away on his quad, when suddenly, they heard a frantic barking coming from the front of the cottage.

"Who could that be?" said Dave. "We don't often get visitors. Woody, could you go round to the front and see who that is please?"

"No problem, Dave," replied Woody, quickly disappearing to the front of Ivy Cottage. There, standing at the gate with her front paws up, trying to open it, was Florence, Graham, the shop owner's lovely Cocker Spaniel.

Woody could speak Dog but Florence was very agitated, dog words tumbling out of her mouth chaotically, and he was having great difficulty understanding her.

"Florence!" Please slow down and speak clearly! I can't understand you," said Woody. "What's wrong?"

With great effort, Florence slowed down and repeated her message. "Please, Woody, is Andy in? My master isn't well. He can't get up from his bed; he won't speak, and he doesn't look good at all. He hasn't eaten all day, and I am really worried about him. Oh dear! Oh dear! I didn't know what to do so I ran up here as fast as I could!"

She was starting to panic again so Woody came in quickly. "Could you just sit there one minute, Florence, and I'll go round and tell the others?"

She vanished instantly around Ivy Cottage and quickly told them the situation. They all rushed round to the front.

"Florence! Andy is away working just now on the quad," said Morag, "but we'll try to find him and tell him what's happened. Then he'll be back very quickly, I can assure you of that. Are you okay with that?"

"Thanks ever so much," croaked Florence. She'd barked so much that her throat was sore.

"Cassie, Kate, Dave! We'll go down to the shop with Florence and see what we can do. Woody! Jerome! Your only instruction is to find Andy as quickly as possible and tell him the situation."

"No problem!" they replied as they spread their wings and disappeared before anyone else moved. They were pretty sure these days where he was likely to be and were gone in an instant. Both were expert fliers.

Florence led the way down to the shop. She always carried herself like royalty with her high-class gait and posture, but now urgently! She was a real charmer. Everyone loved her, and she loved almost everyone.

The only exception had been that cruel and heartless crofter who had chased after Morag and Dave. He had charged into the shop in a bad temper just prior to his 'performance' at Ivy Cottage, giving Graham a rude cross-examination as to 'his' donkeys' whereabouts.

Graham had just blanked him and walked off into the back of the shop. The shop door had slammed just as the bad-tempered crofter had stomped furiously out, uttering a parting obscenity and heading up to Ivy Cottage to try his luck there. Florence disliked him instantly.

Now, she led the way down to the shop. Always classy, now urgently so.

Graham was lying on his bed when they came in, looking up at the ceiling. They all crowded in, donkeys as well, and stood round his bed. He was silent and didn't notice them. They intuitively knew this was not good.

Cassie and Kate jumped gently onto his bed and snuggled in. Graham had always loved them doing this but – no reaction! He just looked at the ceiling. The donkeys put their heads on the bed next to his hands. In the past, he would always stroke their muzzles gently, but again – no reaction.

They all heard Andy's van screech to a halt outside the shop, and shortly after, he was at Graham's bedside. Graham barely acknowledged him.

Andy also noticed it and just one look, that's all it took for Andy to understand. It had happened to him a long time ago. The symptoms were apathy, loss of appetite (what's the point?), lack of communication, an absence of joy and purpose in life and an inability to do any day-to-day mundane jobs that make up the bulk of living.

In short – clinical depression. Brought about by acute loneliness, even though he saw people every day through the shop. That was the paradox.

Andy took his hand and gently stroked it. All the birds and donkeys were around him doing their best to create a loving atmosphere, and it only took a few minutes for Graham to begin to respond, turning his head to look at them all. Andy, while still holding his hand, smiled at him and almost immediately he smiled back.

Andy knew, that instant, that healing had begun and he was determined that Graham wasn't going to 'go down on his watch'. No way.

"Graham," he said in a very soft, gentle voice, "could you possibly sit up, please, if you can. I'll help you. Then why don't we have a lovely cup of tea and we'll talk music if you'd like. I don't know very much about classical piano playing but I would love it if you agree to have me as a pupil."

Graham sat up slowly with Andy's help. Once he was comfortable, Andy held his hand with his own two hands, opened it out and carefully placed his fingers through those of Graham. He gave it a gentle squeeze and softly said, "You have true friends here, Graham. We are all here. Look round about you."

He looked at all the animals and birds, Dave and Morag, Cassie and Kate, Jerome and Woody. There, in the centre of them all, was dear Florence, eyes shining. Their eyes of concern lifted him up inside. He began to gently stroke the hens, donkeys and Florence.

Something had shifted deep down within him and when Andy returned with his favourite Earl Grey Tea and some delicious biscuits, he felt the joy of life flooding back into his soul!

"Could you possibly play something for us, Graham? Something special that you've always loved? It would make our day," said Andy. "If anyone comes for provisions I'll serve them. I know, more or less, how it's done and I'll still hear you from the counter. But remember, Graham, it's okay if you don't fancy it, honestly."

Dear Florence was barking with delight as Chopin's Étude filled the air. She hadn't heard that one for a long time.

Graham's hands flew majestically over the keys. He and his piano became One! Everyone was amazed at the beautiful music being played by an obvious Master of the piano!

He started to speak again. From then on, Graham never looked back. Andy always made a point of giving him a huge hug if he hadn't seen him for a day or two. They both loved it. Not just Graham! And Andy, when he could, helped out Graham as much as he could, with the running of the shop. Although Graham wasn't really aware of it, the benefit was two-way.

Cassie and Kate, Morag and Dave, Jerome and Woody – and especially Florence – all played their part in bringing Graham back from the brink of misery.

There was no doubt that Graham was fragile for a while, but very slowly, he became stronger and stronger in mind, body and spirit. All the animals and birds noticed it, especially dear Florence.

Andy noticed it as well and gave thanks. It fleetingly occurred to him that maybe nothing exists in isolation and nobody is an island. Maybe we live in a world of illusion? Maybe we only see the 'tip of the iceberg'? Yes, maybe that's it!

Andy's pensive moment passed and he remembered that Graham's piano recital was coming up soon at St Minnis Church Hall.

Graham would be ready, he was sure of that!

Chapter Eight

Bad Weather

One Sunday, they all decided to walk to the east side of Stelling Isle. It was a bit of an adventure as the birds had never been there before, and, of course, neither had the donkeys.

"Are you coming as well, Andy?" chirped up Woody, but Andy decided he was too busy with more endless paperwork.

"Don't be back too late," he said, not looking up. His 'demonic' computer screen was 'the boss' just now.

"We won't!" they replied, unaware that fate was conspiring against them! With Cassie and Kate on Dave, and Jerome and Woody on the back of Morag, leading the way, they all set off in good heart.

The weather wasn't settled. In the west, it can blow hard or settle down very quickly. A lovely sunny day can easily change to wind and rain just like that!

The hens were still keen to show off their new flying skills they'd discovered on their journey to the west. They had continued to practise every day on the rocky crags at the back of Ivy Cottage.

"Look at us!" they cried in glee. "Aren't we good?" as they clumsily launched themselves off Dave's back, flapped a few yards and landed close by. They would return to Dave's back with a distinct lack of precision and twice they were unsuccessful and hit his flank square-on.

"Oops, sorry Dave, we didn't mean it!" they apologised. But Dave just looked round, shook his head, and muttered something quietly to Morag in 'broad donkey' that the birds didn't understand. It probably wasn't very complimentary about their flying skills! They both raised and shook their heads vigorously, a kind of 'donkey laugh' and just carried on walking.

It was all a bit of fun. But Woody and Jerome could see that their flying skills were barely up to chick standard. Never mind, they were enjoying themselves!

As they continued, Jerome and Woody scouted ahead and returned with the advice that maybe it wasn't advisable to carry on much farther today. There were cliffs ahead and the wind was beginning to gust strongly.

"Oh, come on Jerome! It can't be that bad!" said Cassie and Kate. "We'll just go and take a look. There's no harm in that, is there?"

"Well, I suppose not," replied Jerome, unconvinced. "Maybe just a quick look."

"Hooray!" shouted the hens, and they all continued slowly to the cliffs. A fateful decision! Soon they were there and the wind was now blowing hard. Cassie and Kate were having a great time getting picked up by the wind and deposited several hundred yards back where the others were watching apprehensively. They seemed to sense danger in the wind, but Cassie and Kate were unaware of any danger and were enjoying 'showing off' to the rest of the on-looking entourage.

Strangely, just at that time, Andy, who was busy repairing a deer fence several miles away, felt a sudden sense of unease and shivered with cold. He couldn't understand it. It felt like an impending doom that persisted. But everything seemed okay!? In the end, he dropped his tools, mounted his works quad – a 4-wheel drive (4WD) all-terrain vehicle (ATV) designed specifically for travel over rough ground, and sped off in the direction he thought he'd last seen his animal and bird friends. He knew they were going east.

His quad, with its balloon tyres, soon gobbled up the two miles. Andy strained his eyes, hoping to see any sign of them, but – nothing! ... Then ... There! He could faintly see Dave and Morag in the distance and knew the birds would be there as well. He felt there was something wrong. He could now hear thunderous braying above the wind as he closed in. Something was definitely wrong!

The donkeys, he could now see, were close to a well-known dangerous cliff edge. When they saw him, they brayed even louder. Andy could tell they were really distressed about something, but what?! In a minute he was there.

"Morag, Dave – what's wrong?" he shouted over the rising wind.

"Andy! Andy! Thank God you're here! Cassie and Kate have gone over the edge!" they answered, panic-stricken.

"What? Try and calm down and tell me what's happened," he said.

"Well, it's awful, Andy. Cassie and Kate were just showing us their new gliding and flying skills and they got blown over the edge. We told them the wind was too gusty and strong but they wouldn't listen. We don't know what to do! Please help, Andy!" they pleaded, both still traumatised.

Suddenly, Jerome and Woody appeared out of the howling wind and gloom. "Thank goodness you're here, Andy!" they cried. "We know where they are but it's impossible to help them. They were blown over the cliff and somehow managed to cling to a ledge not too far down. Cassie looks terrified but okay. Kate isn't responding. I think she is badly injured, Andy. We can't get near; the wind is too strong. There must be something we can do but we can't think of anything. It's terrible!" they cried.

The wind was now shrieking like a banshee, and Andy was suddenly devoid of any solution. What could he do? Nothing! It all seemed hopeless! They were looking to him, and he simply had 'nothing to give'. It all seemed hopeless indeed. He just stood there and looked up. Just darkness!

Then he recognised that same pinprick of light that come to him in the blackness during his journey over from the east of Scotland. He put out his hands in desperation, as if to receive, without thinking, and in his mind the white light flashed in a momentary brilliance and left one word. ROPE. That was all.

Andy suddenly remembered the little storage container at the back of the quad. It contained a considerable length of rope he had saved from his old forestry work. He ran to it quickly, pulled the rope out of storage and manoeuvred the quad into a position close to the cliff edge. He then tied a bowline knot around his waist, held the other end, and slipped the rope around the quad's strong tow bar.

He had decided! He was going down for them! Over the cliff edge! And the weather was getting worse. It was suicidal.

He worked his way carefully over the edge, in the exact spot Woody had said and began, slowly, to work his way down, getting buffeted left and right violently as the wind reached a full gale and still increased. Then the rain started. It was 'Hell on Earth' now.

He looked down through the mayhem and saw them close by. Any moment now they could be blown off their ledge. He descended another three feet and he was there!

As quickly as possible, he picked up Cassie and Kate and, as best as he could, placed them gently inside the front of his jacket. Above the wind he could just hear Cassie repeating the words, "Andy! Andy! Andy!

Andy ...!" Kate's body was limp but still warm. Alive, just.

This was going to be the toughest bit. Going back up. Andy started the upward climb. Now, getting thrown about by the violent wind which seemed to be saying triumphantly, "We've got you now!"

He knew he was tiring quickly, and when he managed to reach just below the cliff edge, he was utterly exhausted and couldn't summon the strength for that final push.

Worse than that! He was beginning to slowly drop back down. Something must be wrong with the rope at the quad end. He couldn't understand it. He was a spent force. He had nobly tried to save his two great bird friends and failed!

At the quad, Morag and Dave quickly saw what was happening. The hand brake was slipping and the quad was slowly moving toward the cliff-edge. It would disappear over it shortly and all would be lost.

They reacted instantly and placed their large bodies in front of the rear wheels and lay down in front of them. The quad stopped slipping back. Then Morag told Dave to grab the rope with his teeth and try pulling Andy up.

Donkeys possess very strong teeth and even stronger willpower. That's why they are sometimes inaccurately described as 'stubborn'. It's their unbreakable will that is stubborn and won't crack even under extreme conditions.

Dave gripped the rope tightly in his mouth and hauled away with all his might. But, as close as he was to succeeding, it wasn't enough. Morag, in command, decided to move quickly from blocking the quad to Dave's side and also grabbed the rope with her teeth. With two jaws clamped shut around the rope. They both dug deep, as donkeys can and hauled on the rope with superhuman strength. Slowly, very slowly, Andy and Cassie and Kate began to rise again to the top of the cliff.

Now they were at the cliff top but even the superhuman donkeys couldn't pull them that last yard over the top to safety. So! So! Close!

Another word flashed momentarily in Andy's head. Foothold! Foothold! It said. He couldn't see anything now down below but just reached out with his foot anywhere. Nothing! But there was! He felt his foot land on a jutting-out piece of rock and, with his last ounce of strength and his red raw hands, hauled himself and his precious birds over the top to safety. They'd done it! They'd done it!

For a minute, all he could do was lie there on his back gasping for breath, completely spent, with Cassie and Kate safely in his jacket.

Everyone crowded around him. Dave and Morag, themselves exhausted, simply glowed with tender love for their great friend and master. Woody the Great Spotted Woodpecker and Jerome the Mallard Duck were joined by Cassie, who had come out of Andy's jacket so thankful and full of beans.

Andy recovered magically! His friends had a profound healing effect on him. He felt it. Pure love. But there was no time to waste!

He checked on Kate, still in his jacket, unconscious. She was still alive, but only just. They had to get back to Ivy Cottage 'pronto' (as quickly as possible!). It was not an evening for being out. A severe storm!

So, with a quick loving hug of Morag and Dave, and in the driving rain, they all dashed back and in the door to warmth and shelter. Andy got the peat fire going quickly, the warm flames so comforting and then he removed Kate, gently, from his jacket.

He placed her carefully on the sofa with warm cushions for support. There was nothing else he could do but keep her warm and comfortable.

She was in God's hands now.

Chapter Nine

New Horizons

Kate suddenly found herself walking down a busy street somewhere. She didn't recognise the place at all. Everything seemed to glow with a surreal golden radiance. Even the street seemed 'paved with gold'! All the beautiful hens she passed looked familiar. Where had she seen them all?

Ah! She remembered! In that awful battery-hen enclosure. Now they looked so clean and happy, their feathers in tip-top condition, clucking away with their friends. Some hens walked with very handsome cockerels wing in wing.

Everyone smiled and the sun shone brightly.

There were small perches on one side of the street for relaxing, chatting to friends, or just watching the world go by. Beyond that, beautiful green fields bordered by mature hardwood trees stretched to the horizon.

On the other side of the street were rows of majestically ornate hen coops. If Kate had looked inside, she would've been stunned by the opulent splendour of the interior décor. It was so spotlessly clean that one could imagine laying 'golden eggs' in such luxurious surroundings.

"Tattie! Can it be you?" exclaimed Kate in surprise as she passed a roadside perch with a magnificent-looking cockerel on it.

"Kate! Kate! Kate! My precious Kate! It is indeed me!" and he jumped off his perch and they warmly embraced, wing wrapped round wing. Wise old Tattie looked anything but old; a magnificent-looking bird again. "I was told to meet you here, Kate, and have a chat about things to come and choices you have to make. There are always new horizons for us all to explore, new realities to experience and new people to love, as I love you. Come, sit with me awhile on this perch, Kate, and we'll chat."

"Oh, please tell me everything, Tattie. I would love to know it all," replied Kate enthusiastically. They touched beaks passionately, a sort of 'hen kiss', and then Tattie continued.

"Hold your horses, Kate!" smiled Tattie. "There are some things we can never know." But Kate couldn't stop.

"Please tell me, Tattie, do we hens have a soul like humans do? Is this the afterlife? What are these New Horizons everyone talks about? Tattie! Tell me! Tell me! Tell me!"

"All in good time, Kate. One question I must ask you, though, is – are you happy in your present earthly life with Andy and the others?"

"Oh yes Tattie, completely happy. I love them and they love me. They are all my dearest friends.

They bring an inner joy to me all the time." Kate was becoming tearful thinking about them.

"Well, if you are happy there, Kate, you can go back to them if you so desire or you can stay here with me and meet new friends." Tattie looked deeply into her eyes, waiting for a reply.

"I have to go back, Tattie. I don't know why. I just feel I have to go. What a joy my earthly friends are. They mean so much to me, and I would love to continue with them, if that's okay?"

"That's perfectly okay, my dearest Kate. I'll always be close by you, and we'll meet again when it's time, but I've got a few things to tell you before you leave us.

"What will happen, Kate, with your decision to go, you will forget that you had to make this choice and willingly submit to total amnesia. It's routine, and it'll make your return much easier. It's a 'tough call' sometimes on the earthly plane and with complete knowledge of this world as well, it would make life doubly difficult for you.

"So you will forget it all, my dearest, but in truth you never can. Just call me any time, and I will come. Now! I will answer one of your many questions before you leave us, Kate.

"These New Horizons are endless but you will enjoy exploring them, looking over them and learning from them as and when they appear! But for now, it's goodbye," and for the last time, they touched tenderly.

Then Kate fell immediately asleep, a beautiful, restful sleep.

Andy sat with her all night. The birds found their comfortable spots around her, and Dave and Morag lay down in the hallway outside. They were all praying hard, in their own way, for their dear friend, Kate. Morning would reveal her answer; they all knew that.

Kate's life hung in the balance that night. Was she in this world or the next?

At first light, Kate's eyes suddenly opened and she breathed in the clean island air once more. She saw Andy and the others watching over her and wondered why.

"What are you all looking at?" she said with a puzzled expression on her face. "Have I slept in? I was just resting awhile. I feel fine!"

Andy looked up to the sky. *Thank you*, he said silently.

"Is there any food to eat, please Andy? I'm feeling rather peckish. And I could do with a drink as well, thanks."

"Of course, my precious. Coming right up!" Andy was a very happy man.

The others were just as happy but said nothing to Kate about what had happened. Kate herself had no idea. Her memory of past events had been erased. She couldn't understand all the attention the birds and donkeys were giving her but loved it immensely anyway.

As she rose and stretched her wings, she thought of her great friend Cassie. Where was she? After eating, Kate walked off to find her, now as fresh as a daisy.

Cassie had quietly slipped away on Kate's return, too overcome with emotion at her dearest friend coming back from the brink. She thought she'd lost her for good!

She was outside in the coop, fully recovered, and when they met again, the heavens rejoiced! Deafening clucks, wing hugs and beak touching were the order of the day. Everyone could hear it! Even in Ivy Cottage.

Normally as keen on her new (but limited!) flying abilities, Kate couldn't understand her loss of interest in it. *Oh well, I'm sure it'll return soon*, she thought, quite unconcerned. *There'll be plenty of other things to do and eggs to lay as well!*

But occasionally, Kate would just stop for a second for no apparent reason and ponder. In that moment, she would glimpse her 'street of gold' again and, as quickly as it had come, it would disappear. What was left was a feeling of wellbeing, of love, of acceptance. She didn't understand it, but that didn't matter.

What had happened was that, in that instant, the veil between worlds had lifted and descended again, as Tattie said it would.

In those fleeting moments, Kate had glimpsed one of her many futures and seen beyond one of her New Horizons.

The End

Epilogue

Queen o'Scots

I feel I must digress for a short while from the 'stars of the show' – Andy and his friends – to mention what is now considered to be an eyesore lying half-buried on Stelling Isle beach next to the harbour: a large, unsightly lump of corroded metal.

To many, it's unrecognisable, something slowly rusting away. What could it be?

Its history, I feel, should be known and its reason for being there.

It was the original ro-ro ferry that served Stelling Isle after the war and was built in the shipyards of Glasgow when Clydeside was one of the major shipbuilding areas of Europe. The ferry was christened *Queen o'Scots* and served Stelling Isle for many years, long before the present causeway was even thought about.

The ferry trip was only half an hour and it would carry most cargo. Cars and lorries were its main customers, but it sometimes included sheep and cattle, really anything transportable! The engines never once broke down. The marine engineer knew his stuff, having come through the war in the merchant navy, so lucky to have survived the Murmansk Run and U-boat threat. It is true to say, though, that in the ferry's long service 'full ahead' was, on rare occasions, really half ahead as one cylinder would 'opt out'!

Captain McTavish was a Skye man and an expert in short crossings. He and his crew knew their jobs inside out, being from the Isle themselves, and they had an almost uncanny ability to predict the weather. They always seemed cheery despite working in some dreadful weather conditions.

McTavish himself could, on occasion, appear sullen, but people who didn't know him always mistook sullenness for a very dry sense of humour. He was, however, a captain with all the responsibilities that came with that title.

He knew the *Queen o'Scots* inside out and what she could and couldn't do. His decision to sail or not to sail was always final, and thus the whole operation worked very well and most efficiently.

Then the 21st century arrived with all the benefits of computerisation and the digital world. Two men in suits arrived from the South – one from the government and the other from the Health & Safety Executive. They spent a whole week looking over the entire operation while tapping their laptops furiously.

It was ominous! The conclusions reached by both men were that the *Queen o'Scots* was too 'analogue' and out-of-date for purpose. Among the many faults were the engines: old-fashioned and in need of a full-time marine engineer.

Even the small on-board toilet didn't escape criticism. The main objections were that, firstly, it was six inches (150mm!) too narrow for 21st-century use and the handwash was still a bar of soap rather than the replacement ferry's dazzling array of modern-day soap dispensers, with compulsory information guide on the wall above.

This initially took the form of a Dutch pre-handwash lotion for softening up those delicate appendages and was, apparently, a blend of secret organic ingredients (according to the guide) brought together in the beautiful bulb fields of the Netherlands. Those involved in its manufacture had to wear clogs for fear of contamination!

Then there was the Norwegian hand cleanser; prepared by hand in the pure Norwegian fjords and containing a wild mountain thyme additive.

This was followed by the post-cleansing, high alpine Swiss conditioner made at altitude by Benedictine monks and containing several closely guarded magical ingredients. Only one has been 'leaked out' to the general public over the years. That of Edelweiss!

Finally, the special Italian hand sanitiser had to be applied for full hand protection. It contained a rare organic pasta formula known only to those at the highest level of Italian society.

Let's face it! One could enjoy a relaxing trip around Europe while 'sitting on the throne'!

Concluding the lavatorial perceptions, the toilet seat was condemned for being slightly the wrong shape for 21st-century posteriors and uncomfortable to use. (Presumably they tried it out!)

In short, the *Queen o'Scots* – nicknamed locally as *SS Dependable* – was decommissioned out-of-service and reduced to a rusting hulk in Stelling Isle harbour. It was replaced by a brand new 'all singing, all dancing' touchscreen ferry built in the Philippines and originally designed for their islands.

Captain McTavish and many of his crew decided to retire and were replaced by a more 'economically viable' foreign captain and crew. Out with the old, in with the new! No problem there!

But unfortunately, more often than not, it couldn't sail due to adverse weather conditions. Apparently, it wasn't quite the right design of the hull for Scottish west coast waters. It continually broke down due to computer software problems, was a complete disaster and a huge waste of money. It just didn't deliver.

The decision was made, after so many delays and cancellations, to stop the ferry service completely and build the causeway we see today. (The same causeway that eventually re-united Andy and his beloved bird friends).

The digital ferry only lasted ten years. It really wasn't 'fit for purpose' and disappeared down south to work in more suitable conditions while *Queen o'Scots* looked on from Stelling Isle harbour, now a sad, rusting hulk. She drifted slowly, over the years, from harbour to beach – a stripped-out empty shell, lost in time.

So, my lovely readers, all I ask of you is to maybe spare a thought for that sad heap of half-buried rusting metal for, in a previous incarnation, it was once a noble, hard-working ferry with an equally noble captain and crew, giving over half a century of invaluable service to the people of Stelling Isle.

Thank you.

"The Stars of the Show"

Andy

Jerome (Mallard Duck)

Cassie & Kate (Hens)

Morag & Dave (Donkeys)

Woody (Great Spotted Woodpecker)

Tattie (Cockerel)